Waldo, Tell Me About Guardian Angels

WALDO, TELL ME ABOUT GUARDIAN ANGELS

First published in the USA by C. Gibson Company, Norwalk, CT06856.

Commonwealth addition by Word (UK) Ltd. 1990.

Printed and bound in Singapore by Times Offset Pte Ltd

ISBN 0-85009-279-5

WORD PUBLISHING

WORD (UK) Ltd
Milton Keynes, England

WORD AUSTRALIA
Kilsyth, Victoria, Australia

STRUIK CHRISTIAN BOOKS (PTY) LTD
Maitland, South Africa

ALBY COMMERCIAL ENTERPRISES PTE LTD
Balmoral Road, Singapore

CHRISTIAN MARKETING NEW ZEALAND LTD
Havelock North, New Zealand

JENSCO LTD
Hong Kong

SALVATION BOOK CENTRE
Malaysia

Waldo, Tell Me About Guardian Angels

by Hans Wilhelm

Word Publishing
Milton Keynes
England

It was a fine summer day. The
perfect day for Michael and his
best friend, Waldo, to try out
Michael's new soapbox car. They
were looking forward to an
exciting ride.

As they started to pick up
speed, Waldo shouted, "I don't
think we should go down this hill.
It's too ST—E—E—P!"

But Michael wasn't listening. He was
too busy steering.

"Waldo!" cried Michael, "Do we have guardian angels?"

"Of course we do!" shouted Waldo as he curled his toes around the bottom of his seat.

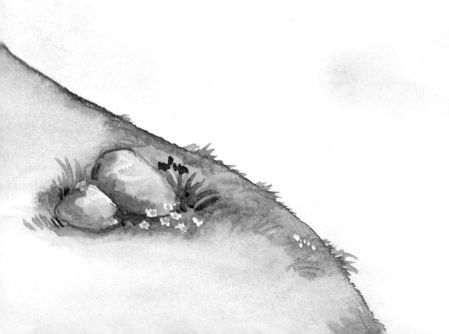

"I think we need one right now!"
yelled Michael as they tumbled down
the slope.

They landed with a big THUD.

"Guardian angels don't protect us
from the silly things we do,"
said Waldo.

"Waldo, tell me about
guardian angels."

"Well, guardian angels warn us not
to do silly things like this."

"I didn't hear a guardian angel warn me as we came down the hill. Did you?" asked Michael.

"You can't hear your guardian angel with your ears. You *feel* his warning."

"How?" asked Michael.

"With your heart," replied Waldo. "Did you ever notice that when you are about to do something wrong or get into trouble, a kind of feeling comes over you? Some people might call it your conscience. But this feeling is from your guardian angel who is talking to you."

"But what if I don't listen?" asked Michael.
"Then you may get hurt, sooner or later."

"Why don't they stop us, if they know that we're going to hurt ourselves?"

"Because God gives us the freedom to choose to do the right thing or the wrong thing. Guardian angels don't interfere with that. They only warn us if we are heading in the wrong direction."

Michael thought for a moment.
He was about to ask Waldo a
question when he saw something
yellow flit by. "Oh, look! A butterfly.
I'm going to catch it."

Michael left Waldo in the tall grass and
ran after the butterfly. It danced
from flower to flower with Michael
right behind.

"Got you!" exclaimed Michael, as he scooped up the butterfly in his hands.

Waldo looked at Michael with sad eyes. "You aren't *really* happy that you've caught that poor butterfly, are you?"

"Why shouldn't I be happy?" demanded Michael.

"Well, what does your heart say? Doesn't it tell you that it's wrong to harm another creature?"

Michael frowned. "Maybe it does…a little."

"A little is enough to make another choice."

"OK," said Michael. Slowly he opened his hands and threw them up toward the sky. "Go home, Little Butterfly."

He laughed as the little butterfly dipped and twirled toward the sun.

Waldo was happy as he watched the smile on Michael's face.

"I do feel happy now," said Michael. "The butterfly is happy and so am I."

"And so am I," laughed Waldo.

"Your guardian angel is happy, too."

"How do you know, Waldo?"

"Can't you *feel* it? I can see it. It shows."

"It does?" whispered Michael.

"Yes," said Waldo. "When you make the right choice, your guardian angel dances with joy."

"And I can feel my angel's joy," interrupted Michael. "I got my happy feeling from my angel."

The two friends played in the warm sun.

After a while, Michael asked,
"Who is my guardian angel?"

"Guardian angels are children
of God, just like you are,"
replied Waldo.

"You mean like a brother or sister?"

"That's right. God gave you a
guardian angel to look after you. God
loves you so much that He doesn't
want you to feel alone or lost."

"I'll *never* feel alone with my
guardian angel near me," said
Michael. "That's a good feeling."

"Should I thank my guardian angel
for helping me?" asked Michael.
"Why don't you thank God for
looking after you in so many ways.
Thank Him for watching over you.
That would make your guardian
angel very, very happy."

    The two friends rocked slowly on
the swing.
    "Waldo," said Michael. "I'll try to
listen more to my guardian angel
from now on."
    Waldo patted Michael on his
shoulder and the friends continued
to swing.